Winnie-the-Pooh's Birthday Book

A. A. MILNE

Winnie-the-Pooh's Birthday Book

WITH DECORATIONS BY
ERNEST H. SHEPARD

Dutton Children's Books
NEW YORK

As Eeyore says, "What are birthdays? Here today and gone tomorrow." So let us make a note of them while we can. Of course it would be pleasanter if other people made a note of ours in their books, rather than called attention to their own in ours, but, even so, if we are careful to write to our Uncle Henry for the 20th of October, wishing him many happy returns, and mentioning casually the coincidence that our birthday is exactly seventeen days later than his, we may find ourselves in the pleasing position of having to write to him again before November is out.

If you buy this book at all, or if anybody gives it to you, it can only be because you are friendly with the four books from which the mottoes have been taken. If that is so, then you can amuse yourself (when you've got *absolutely* nothing to do) by trying to guess from which chapter or verse of a book each quotation comes. With some you will have no difficulty; others will baffle you for a long time, even if you start looking through the books carefully for them. But, of course, if the sun is shining and you can do anything else, I should strongly advise you to do it.

A.A.M.
1931

January

The wind had dropped, and the snow, tired of rushing round in circles trying to catch itself up, now fluttered gently down until it found a place on which to rest, and sometimes the place was Pooh's nose and sometimes it wasn't, and in a little while Piglet was wearing a white muffler round his neck and feeling more snowy behind the ears than he had ever felt before.

The House At Pooh Corner

1

"I only came to oblige. But here I am."
Winnie-the-Pooh

2

On Tuesday, when it hails and snows,
The feeling on me grows and grows
That hardly anybody knows
If those are these or these are those.
Winnie-the-Pooh

3

O Timothy Tim
   Has ten pink toes,
   And ten pink toes
Has Timothy Tim.
   Now We Are Six

4

She would do a Good Thing to Do without thinking
about it. *Winnie-the-Pooh*

5

"What would I do?" I said to Pooh,
"If it wasn't for you," and Pooh said: "True."
Now We Are Six

6

"Pooh!" cried Piglet, and now it was *his* turn to be the admiring one. "You've saved us!"
The House At Pooh Corner

7

"What sort of stories does he like?"
"About himself. Because he's *that* sort of Bear."
Winnie-the-Pooh

8

If I were Emperors,
If I were Kings,
It couldn't be fuller
Of wonderful things.
Now We Are Six

9

It was just the day for Organizing Something, or for Writing a Notice Signed Rabbit.

The House At Pooh Corner

10

It doesn't seem to matter,
If I don't get any fatter
(And I *don't* get any fatter),
What I do.
The House At Pooh Corner

11

"Nobody,
My darling,
Could call me
A fussy man."
When We Were Very Young

12

They heard a deep gruff voice saying in a singing voice that the more it snowed the more it went on snowing and a small high voice tiddely-pomming in between.

The House At Pooh Corner

13

What has she got in that little brown head?
Wonderful thoughts which can never be said.
Now We Are Six

14

The snow, tired of rushing round in circles trying to catch itself up, now fluttered gently down.
The House At Pooh Corner

15

"If you go on making faces like Piglet's, you will grow up to *look* like Piglet."
Winnie-the-Pooh

16

"I was BOUNCED," said Eeyore.
The House At Pooh Corner

17

"He doesn't use long, difficult words, like Owl."
The House At Pooh Corner

18

"Perhaps it's some relation of Pooh's."
Winnie-the-Pooh

19

"You'll be quite safe with *him*."
Winnie-the-Pooh

20

When Anne and I go out a walk,
We hold each other's hand and talk
Of all the things we mean to do
When Anne and I are forty-two.
Now We Are Six

21

"I don't hold with all this washing. . . . This modern Behind-the-ears nonsense."   *Winnie-the-Pooh*

22

"The only reason for making honey is so as *I* can eat it."   *Winnie-the-Pooh*

23

He gets what exercise he can
By falling off the ottoman.
   When We Were Very Young

24

"I must find one of those Clever Readers who can read things."   *Winnie-the-Pooh*

25

And the look in his eye
Seemed to say to the sky,
"Now, how to amuse them today?"
Now We Are Six

26

I don't much mind if it rains or snows,
'Cos I've got a lot of honey on my nice
new nose.   *Winnie-the-Pooh*

27

"Enjoy yourself."
    "I am," said Pooh.
    "Some can," said Eeyore.
        Winnie-the-Pooh

28

Oh, I like his way of talking,
    Yes, I do.
It's the nicest way of talking
    Just for two.
The House At Pooh Corner

29

"A little Consideration, a little Thought for Others, makes all the difference."
Winnie-the-Pooh

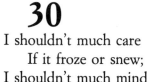

30

I shouldn't much care
If it froze or snew;
I shouldn't much mind
If it snowed or friz.
Now We Are Six

31

Winnie-the-Pooh sat down at the foot of the tree, put his head between his paws and began to think.
Winnie-the-Pooh

February

The more it
SNOWS-tiddely-pom,
The more it
GOES-tiddely-pom
The more it
GOES-tiddely-pom
On
Snowing.
The House At Pooh Corner

1

"Tracks," said Piglet. "Do you think it's a—a—a Woozle?"

Winnie-the-Pooh

2

If I were John and John were Me,
Then he'd be six and I'd be three.

Now We Are Six

3

"It's snowing still," said Eeyore gloomily. "*And freezing.*"

The House At Pooh Corner

4

"I have been Foolish and Deluded," said Pooh, "and I am a Bear of No Brain at All."

Winnie-the-Pooh

5

"Going on an Expotition?" said Pooh eagerly. "I don't think I've ever been on one of those."

Winnie-the-Pooh

6

If anybody mentioned Hums or Trees or String or Storms-in-the-Night, Piglet's nose went all pink at the tip. 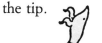 *The House At Pooh Corner*

7

They went to the Six Pine Trees, and threw fir-cones at each other until they had forgotten what they came for.

The House At Pooh Corner

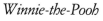

8

Where am I going? I don't quite know.
Down to the stream where the king-cups grow.

When We Were Very Young

9

He didn't feel very brave, for the word which was really jiggeting about in his brain was "Heffalumps."

Winnie-the-Pooh

10

"Nobody tells me," said Eeyore. "Nobody keeps me Informed. I make it seventeen days come Friday since anybody spoke to me." *The House At Pooh Corner*

11

"It is because you are a very small animal that you will be Useful in the adventure before us."

Winnie-the-Pooh

12

"I've got two names," said Christopher Robin carelessly.

Winnie-the-Pooh

13

"Well, that's funny," he thought. "I wonder what that bang was."

Winnie-the-Pooh

14

"Oh, Bear!" said Christopher Robin. "How I do love you!"

Winnie-the-Pooh

15

A Thought. If Roo had jumped out of Kanga's pocket and Piglet had jumped in, Kanga wouldn't know the difference.

Winnie-the-Pooh

16

"Sillies, I went and saw the Queen. She says my hands are *purfickly* clean!"

When We Were Very Young

17

And nobody KNOWS-tiddely-pom,
How cold my TOES-tiddely-pom
How cold my TOES-tiddely-pom
Are growing.

The House At Pooh Corner

18

"There are twelve pots of honey in my cupboard, and they've been calling to me for hours."

The House At Pooh Corner

19

"Yes," said Owl, looking Wise and Thoughtful. "I see what you mean. Undoubtedly."

The House At Pooh Corner

20

There once was a Dormouse who lived in a bed
Of delphiniums (blue) and geraniums (red).

When We Were Very Young

21

"Piglet," said Rabbit, taking out a pencil, and licking the end of it, "you haven't any pluck." *Winnie-the-Pooh*

22

The Piglet lived in a very grand house in the middle of a beech-tree. *Winnie-the-Pooh*

23

If he let go of the string, he would fall—*bump*—and he didn't like the idea of that. *Winnie-the-Pooh*

24

"I am *not* Roo," said Piglet loudly. "I am Piglet!" *Winnie-the-Pooh*

25

Eeyore nodded gloomily. "It will rain soon, you see if it doesn't," he said.

Winnie-the-Pooh

26

Tattoo was the mother of Pinkle Purr,
A little black nothing of feet and fur.

Now We Are Six

27

"Owl," said Pooh, "I have thought of something."
    "Astute and Helpful Bear," said Owl.

The House At Pooh Corner

28

He felt sure that a Very Clever Brain could catch a Heffalump if only he knew the right way to go about it.

Winnie-the-Pooh

29

So he took hold of Pooh's front paws and Rabbit took
hold of Christopher Robin, and all Rabbit's friends and
relations took hold of Rabbit, and they all pulled
together.   *Winnie-the-Pooh*

March

Binker isn't greedy, but he does like things to eat,
So I have to say to people when they're giving
    me a sweet,
"Oh, Binker wants a chocolate, so could you give
    me two?"
And then I eat it for him, 'cos his teeth are rather
    new.

Now We Are Six

1

"I don't know if you are interested in Poetry at all?"
    "Hardly at all," said Kanga.   *Winnie-the-Pooh*

2

"Pooh!" he whispered.
    "Yes, Piglet?"
    "Nothing," said Piglet, taking Pooh's paw. "I just wanted to be sure of you."

The House At Pooh Corner

3

Cottleston, Cottleston, Cottleston Pie,
A fish can't whistle and neither can I.
                    Winnie-the-Pooh

4

"Don't Bustle me," said Eeyore, getting up slowly.
"Don't now-then me."

The House At Pooh Corner

5

Pooh, who had gone into a happy dream, woke up with a start, and said that Honey was a much more trappy thing than Haycorns. *Winnie-the-Pooh*

6

"You're the Best Bear in All the World," said Christopher Robin soothingly. *Winnie-the-Pooh*

7

He was getting rather tired by this time, so that is why he sang a Complaining Song. *Winnie-the-Pooh*

8

"I wish I could jump like that," he thought. "Some can and some can't. That's how it is." *Winnie-the-Pooh*

9

They were all quite happy when Pooh and Piglet came along, and they stopped working in order to have a little rest and listen to Pooh's new song.

The House At Pooh Corner

10

Owl coughed in an unadmiring sort of way, and said that, if Pooh was sure that *was* all, they could now give their minds to the Problem of Escape.

The House At Pooh Corner

11

The sun was so delightfully warm that Pooh had almost decided to go on being Pooh in the middle of the stream for the rest of the morning.

The House At Pooh Corner

12

"Without Pooh," said Rabbit solemnly as he sharpened his pencil, "the adventure would be impossible."

Winnie-the-Pooh

13

"Where are we going?" said Pooh, hurrying after him, and wondering whether it was to be an Explore or a What-shall-I-do-about-you-know-what.

The House At Pooh Corner

14

"Bother!" said Pooh. "It all comes of trying to be kind to Heffalumps." And he got back into bed.

Winnie-the-Pooh

15

Piglet thought that they ought to have a Reason for going to see everybody, like Looking for Small or Organizing an Expotition, if Pooh could think of something.   *The House At Pooh Corner*

16

"I am calling it this," said Owl importantly, and he showed them what he had been making. It was a square piece of board with the name of the house painted on it.   *The House At Pooh Corner*

17

"Rabbit," said Pooh to himself. "I *like* talking to Rabbit. He uses short, easy words, like 'What about lunch?'"   *The House At Pooh Corner*

18

"A party for Me?" thought Pooh to himself. "How grand!"   *Winnie-the-Pooh*

19

They're changing guard at Buckingham Palace— Christopher Robin went down with Alice.
          When We Were Very Young

20

The wind was against them now, and Piglet's ears streamed behind him like banners.
          The House At Pooh Corner

21

Binker isn't greedy, but he does like things to eat.

Now We Are Six

22

Owl felt that it was rather beneath him to talk about little cake things with pink sugar icing.

Winnie-the-Pooh

23

There were Two little Bears who lived in a Wood,
And one of them was Bad and the other was Good.

Now We Are Six

24

"Owl," said Rabbit shortly, "you and I have brains. The others have fluff." *The House At Pooh Corner*

25

Of all the Knights in Appledore
  The wisest was Sir Thomas Tom.
                    Now We Are Six

26

The more Tigger put his nose into this and his paw into that, the more things he found which Tiggers didn't like.   *The House At Pooh Corner*

27

"What do Jagulars do?" asked Piglet, hoping that they wouldn't.   *The House At Pooh Corner*

28

Pooh's first idea was that they should dig a Very Deep Pit, and then the Heffalump would come along and fall into the Pit.   *Winnie-the-Pooh*

29

"Suppose *I* carried *my* family about with me in *my* pocket, how many pockets should I want?"

Winnie-the-Pooh

30

It didn't look at all like a house now; it looked like a tree which had been blown down; and as soon as a house looks like that, it is time you tried to find another one.   *The House At Pooh Corner*

31

When Winnie-the-Pooh came stumping along, Eeyore was very glad to be able to stop thinking for a little, in order to say "How do you do?" in a gloomy manner.

Winnie-the-Pooh

April

Piglet was busy digging a small hole in the ground outside his house.

"Hallo, Piglet," said Pooh.

"Hallo, Pooh," said Piglet, giving a jump of surprise. "I knew it was you."

"So did I," said Pooh. "What are you doing?"

"I'm planting a haycorn, Pooh, so that it can grow up into an oak-tree, and have lots of haycorns just outside the front door instead of having to walk miles and miles, do you see, Pooh?"

The House At Pooh Corner

1

"And if anyone knows anything about anything," said Bear to himself, "it's Owl who knows something about something."

Winnie-the-Pooh

2

Pooh looked at his two paws. He knew that when you had decided which one of them was the right, then the other one was the left.

The House At Pooh Corner

3

"You're taking up a good deal of room in my house—*do* you mind if I use your back legs as a towel-horse?"

Winnie-the-Pooh

4

Here is Edward Bear, coming downstairs now, bump, bump, bump, on the back of his head.

Winnie-the-Pooh

5

The Piglet was sitting on the ground at the door of his house blowing happily at a dandelion, and wondering whether it would be this year, next year, sometime or never.

Winnie-the-Pooh

6

And there I saw a white swan make
Another white swan in the lake.
When We Were Very Young

7

This warm and sunny Spot
　　Belongs to Pooh.
And here he wonders what
　　He's going to do.
The House At Pooh Corner

8

What is the matter with Mary Jane?
She's crying with all her might and main.
When We Were Very Young

9

"It's like this," Pooh said. "When you go after honey with a balloon, the great thing is not to let the bees know you're coming." *Winnie-the-Pooh*

10

She wore her yellow sun-bonnet,
  She wore her greenest gown;
She turned to the south wind
  And curtsied up and down.
When We Were Very Young

11

"What's twice eleven?" I said to Pooh.
("Twice what?" said Pooh to Me.)
Now We Are Six

12

Next to Piglet's house was a piece of broken board which had: "TRESPASSERS W" on it.
Winnie-the-Pooh

13

Piglet explained to Tigger that he mustn't mind what Eeyore said because he was *always* gloomy.

The House At Pooh Corner

14

"It's a little Anxious," Piglet said to himself, "to be a Very Small Animal Entirely Surrounded by Water."

Winnie-the-Pooh

15

Here I go up in my swing
    Ever so high.
I am the King of the fields, and the King
    Of the town.   *Now We Are Six*

16

"I'm planting a haycorn, Pooh, so that it can grow up into an oak-tree, and have lots of haycorns just outside the front door."   *The House At Pooh Corner*

17

Christopher Robin had wheezles and sneezles,
They bundled him into his bed.

Now We Are Six

18

Pooh felt that the Heffalump was as good as caught
already.

Winnie-the-Pooh

19

"We're all going on an Expotition with Christopher
Robin!"

"What is it when we're on it?"

"A sort of boat, I think," said Pooh.

Winnie-the-Pooh

20

Between the woods the afternoon
Is fallen in a golden swoon,
The sun looks down from quiet skies
To where a quiet water lies.

When We Were Very Young

21

"Help, help!" cried Piglet, "a Heffalump, a Horrible Heffalump!"
Winnie-the-Pooh

22

"When you suddenly go into somebody's house, and he says, 'Hallo, Pooh, you're just in time for a little smackerel of something,' then it's what I call a Friendly Day."
The House At Pooh Corner

23

"Poetry and Hums aren't things which you get, they're things which get *you*."
The House At Pooh Corner

24

"Is anybody at home?" called out Pooh very loudly. "No!" said a voice.
Winnie-the-Pooh

25

Owl was telling Kanga an Interesting Anecdote full of long words like Encyclopædia and Rhododendron.

Winnie-the-Pooh

26

Now it happened that Kanga had felt rather motherly that morning, and Wanting to Count Things.

The House At Pooh Corner

27

"Owl! I require an answer! It's Bear speaking."

Winnie-the-Pooh

28

"I shouldn't be surprised if it hailed a good deal tomorrow," Eeyore was saying. "Blizzards and what-not."

The House At Pooh Corner

29

Small's real name was Very Small Beetle, but he was called Small for short, when he was spoken to at all.

The House At Pooh Corner

30

"Pooh," said Rabbit kindly, "you haven't any brain."
"I know," said Pooh humbly.   *Winnie-the-Pooh*

May

Piglet had got up early that morning to pick himself a bunch of violets; and when he had picked them and put them in a pot in the middle of his house, it suddenly came over him that nobody had ever picked Eeyore a bunch of violets, and the more he thought of this, the more he thought how sad it was to be an Animal who had never had a bunch of violets picked for him.

The House At Pooh Corner

1

"Somebody's making a buzzing-noise, and the only reason for making a buzzing-noise that *I* know of is because you're a bee." *Winnie-the-Pooh*

2

Roo was washing his face and paws in the stream, while Kanga explained to everybody proudly that this was the first time he had ever washed his face himself.

Winnie-the-Pooh

3

"The fact is," said Rabbit, "you're stuck."

Winnie-the-Pooh

4

"How long does getting thin take?" asked Pooh anxiously. *Winnie-the-Pooh*

5

Eeyore stood by himself in a thistly corner of the forest and thought about things. *Winnie-the-Pooh*

6

Pooh was sitting in his house one day, counting his pots of honey. *The House At Pooh Corner*

7

"Tigger is all right *really*," said Piglet lazily.
The House At Pooh Corner

8

"We're going to discover the North Pole."
"Oh!" said Pooh. "What *is* the North Pole?"
Winnie-the-Pooh

9

"I am a Bear of Very Little Brain, and long words Bother me."

Winnie-the-Pooh

10

"Christopher Robin gave me a mastershalum seed, and I planted it, and I'm going to have mastershalums all over the front door."

The House At Pooh Corner

11

"Good-bye," said Eeyore. "Mind you don't get blown away, little Piglet. You'd be missed."

The House At Pooh Corner

12

On Monday, when the sun is hot
I wonder to myself a lot.

Winnie-the-Pooh

13

One day when he felt that he couldn't wait any longer,
Rabbit brained out a Notice.

The House At Pooh Corner

14

Along the narrow carpet ride,
With primroses on either side,
Between their shadows and the sun,
The cows came slowly, one by one.

When We Were Very Young

15

Wherever I am, there's always Pooh,
There's always Pooh and Me.

Now We Are Six

16

Pooh went to the larder; and he stood on a chair, and
took down a very large jar of honey.

Winnie-the-Pooh

17

Of course Pooh would be with him, and it was much more Friendly with two. *Winnie-the-Pooh*

18

As they went, Tigger told Roo (who wanted to know) all about the things that Tiggers could do.

The House At Pooh Corner

19

It suddenly came over him that nobody had ever picked Eeyore a bunch of violets. *The House At Pooh Corner*

20

Piglet trotted off home as quickly as he could, very glad to be Out of All Danger again. *Winnie-the-Pooh*

21

Piglet told himself that never in all his life, and *he* was goodness knows *how* old—three, was it, or four?—never had he seen so much rain. *Winnie-the-Pooh*

22

Nobody seemed to know where they came from, but there they were in the Forest: Kanga and Baby Roo. *Winnie-the-Pooh*

23

"My spelling is Wobbly," said Pooh. "It's good spelling but it Wobbles." *Winnie-the-Pooh*

24

Isn't it funny
How a bear likes honey?
Buzz! Buzz! Buzz!
I wonder why he does?
Winnie-the-Pooh

25

Christopher Robin goes
Hoppity, hoppity,
Hoppity, hoppity, hop.
When We Were Very Young

26

Owl, wise though he was in many ways, somehow went all to pieces over delicate words like MEASLES and BUTTERED TOAST.   *Winnie-the-Pooh*

27

Pooh had made up a little hum that very morning, as he was doing his Stoutness Exercises in front of the glass.
Winnie-the-Pooh

28

"It's a funny thing," said Rabbit ten minutes later, "how everything looks the same in a mist."
The House At Pooh Corner

29

"Would you read a Sustaining Book, such as would help and comfort a Wedged Bear in Great Tightness?"

Winnie-the-Pooh

30

"Do you know what A means, little Piglet?"
"No, Eeyore, I don't."

The House At Pooh Corner

31

When you are a Bear of Very Little Brain, and you Think of Things, you find sometimes that a Thing which seemed very Thingish inside you is quite different when it gets out into the open.   *The House At Pooh Corner*

June

Pooh took his largest pot of honey and escaped with it to a broad branch of his tree, well above the water, and then he climbed down again and escaped with another pot . . . and when the whole Escape was finished, there was Pooh sitting on his branch, dangling his legs, and there, beside him, were ten pots of honey.

Winnie-the-Pooh

1

"And how are you?" said Winnie-the-Pooh.

"Not very how," Eeyore said. "I don't seem to have felt at all how for a long time."
Winnie-the-Pooh

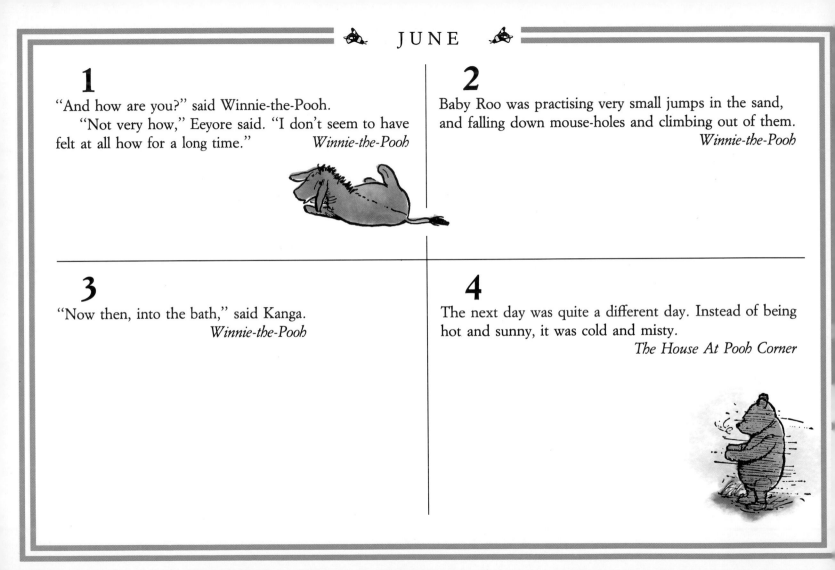

2

Baby Roo was practising very small jumps in the sand, and falling down mouse-holes and climbing out of them.
Winnie-the-Pooh

3

"Now then, into the bath," said Kanga.
Winnie-the-Pooh

4

The next day was quite a different day. Instead of being hot and sunny, it was cold and misty.
The House At Pooh Corner

5

Half way between Pooh's house and Piglet's house was a Thoughtful Spot. *The House At Pooh Corner*

6

Then they had a Very Nearly tea, which is one you forget about afterwards.

The House At Pooh Corner

7

"Nobody can be uncheered with a balloon."
Winnie-the-Pooh

8

"Sing Ho! for the life of a Bear!"
Winnie-the-Pooh

9

Christopher Robin finished the mouthful he was eating and said carelessly: "I saw a Heffalump to-day, Piglet."

Winnie-the-Pooh

10

He and Piglet had fallen into a Heffalump Trap for Poohs! That was what it was.

The House At Pooh Corner

11

"Where are you?" cried Pooh.

"Underneath," said Piglet in an underneath sort of way.

"Underneath what?"

"You," squeaked Piglet.

The House At Pooh Corner

12

I had a penny,
A bright new penny,
I took my penny
   To the market square.
When We Were Very Young

13

"Hallo!" said Tigger. "I've found somebody just like me. I thought I was the only one of them."

The House At Pooh Corner

14

He thought he would begin the Hunt by looking for Piglet, and asking him what they were looking for before he looked for it.

The House At Pooh Corner

15

"I suppose none of you are sitting on a thistle by any chance?"

Winnie-the-Pooh

16

"How do you do Nothing?" asked Pooh.

The House At Pooh Corner

17

I've got shoes with grown up laces,
I've got knickers and a pair of braces.
When We Were Very Young

18

"We're going to discover a Pole or something. Or was it a Mole?"
Winnie-the-Pooh

19

It rained, and it rained, and it rained, and he slept and he slept and he slept.
Winnie-the-Pooh

20

"Sometimes it's a Boat, and sometimes it's more of an Accident. It all depends."
Winnie-the-Pooh

21

"Well," said Pooh, "if I plant a honeycomb outside my house, then it will grow up into a beehive."

The House At Pooh Corner

22

"It isn't much fun for One, but Two Can stick together," says Pooh, says he. "That's how it is," says Pooh.

Now We Are Six

23

Pooh took his largest pot of honey and escaped with it to a broad branch of his tree. *Winnie-the-Pooh*

24

Every Tuesday Kanga spent the day with her great friend Pooh, teaching him to jump.

Winnie-the-Pooh

25

Pooh was getting rather tired of that sand-pit, and suspected it of following them about, because they always ended up at it.

The House At Pooh Corner

26

He could spell his own name WOL, and he could spell Tuesday so that you knew it wasn't Wednesday.

The House At Pooh Corner

27

Pooh was so busy not looking where he was going that he stepped on a piece of the Forest which had been left out by mistake.

The House At Pooh Corner

28

"We'll see," said Kanga.

"You're always seeing, and nothing ever happens," said Roo sadly.

The House At Pooh Corner

29

Although Eating Honey *was* a very good thing to do, there was a moment just before you began to eat it which was better. *The House At Pooh Corner*

30

Owl lived at The Chestnuts, an old-world residence of great charm. *Winnie-the-Pooh*

July

Where is Anne?
    Head above the buttercups,
Walking by the stream,
    Down among the buttercups.
Where is Anne?
Walking with her man,
Lost in a dream,
    Lost among the buttercups.
                Now We Are Six

1

Kanga slipped the medicine spoon in, and then patted him on the back and told him that it was really quite a nice taste when you got used to it.   *Winnie-the-Pooh*

2

He had forgotten to ask who Small was, and whether he was the sort of friend-and-relation who settled on one's nose, or the sort who got trodden on by mistake.

The House At Pooh Corner

3

James James Morrison Morrison
Weatherby George Dupree
Took great care of his Mother,
Though he was only three.
When We Were Very Young

4

"It is the best way to write poetry, letting things come."
The House At Pooh Corner

5

I went down to the shouting sea,
Taking Christopher down with me.
When We Were Very Young

6

"What I like best in the whole world is Me and Piglet
going to see You." *The House At Pooh Corner*

7

"I was walking along, looking for somebody, and then
suddenly I wasn't any more."

The House At Pooh Corner

8

Pooh explained that Piglet was a Very Small Animal
who didn't like bouncing, and asked Tigger not to be
too Bouncy just at first.

The House At Pooh Corner

9

"I shall sing that first line twice, and perhaps I shall find myself singing the third and fourth lines before I have time to think of them."

Winnie-the-Pooh

10

Some think that John boy
Is lost on the hill;
Some say he won't come back,
Some say he will.

Now We Are Six

11

They went on, feeling just a little anxious now, in case the three animals in front of them were of Hostile Intent.

Winnie-the-Pooh

12

"It isn't as easy as I thought. I suppose that's why Heffalumps hardly *ever* get caught."

Winnie-the-Pooh

13

"Many a bear going out on a warm day like this would never have thought of bringing a little something with him." *Winnie-the-Pooh*

14

Tigger was a Very Bouncy Animal, with a way of saying How-do-you-do, which always left your ears full of sand. *The House At Pooh Corner*

15

Rabbit said in a loud voice "In you go, Roo!" and in jumped Piglet into Kanga's pocket.

Winnie-the-Pooh

16

Pooh had had that sinking feeling before, and he knew what it meant. *He was hungry.* *Winnie-the-Pooh*

17

"How did you get here, Pooh?" asked Christopher Robin.

"On my boat," said Pooh proudly.

Winnie-the-Pooh

18

"I shall call this boat *The Brain of Pooh,*" said Christopher Robin.   *Winnie-the-Pooh*

19

"The news has worked through to my corner of the Forest—the damp bit down on the right which nobody wants."   *The House At Pooh Corner*

20

Where is Anne?
     Head above the buttercups,
Walking by the stream,
     Down among the buttercups.
Now We Are Six

21

"Christopher Robin and I are going for a Short Walk,"
Eeyore said, "not a Jostle."

The House At Pooh Corner

22

"I could call this place Poohanpiglet Corner if Pooh
Corner didn't sound better, which it does."

The House At Pooh Corner

23

I found a little beetle, so that Beetle was
    his name,
And I called him Alexander and he answered
    just the same.   *Now We Are Six*

24

"Do you see, Pooh? Do you see, Piglet? Brains first and
then Hard Work."   *The House At Pooh Corner*

25

"Do Tiggers like honey?"

"They like everything," said Tigger cheerfully.

The House At Pooh Corner

26

The Forest was full of gentle sounds, which all seemed to be saying to Pooh, "Don't listen to Rabbit, listen to me."

The House At Pooh Corner

27

"Nobody," he whimpered,
"Could call me a fussy man;
I *only* want a little bit
Of butter for my bread!"

When We Were Very Young

28

"The question is, What are we to do about Kanga?"

Winnie-the-Pooh

29

Pooh thought how wonderful it would be to have a Real Brain.   *The House At Pooh Corner*

30

"I don't want to mention it, but I just mention it. I don't want to complain but there it is. My tail's cold."
                                        Winnie-the-Pooh

31

"I *know* I'm not getting fatter, but his front door may be getting thinner."   *The House At Pooh Corner*

August

"I say, Owl," said Christopher Robin, "isn't this fun? I'm on an island!"

"The atmospheric conditions have been very unfavourable lately," said Owl.

"The what?"

"It has been raining," explained Owl.

"Yes," said Christopher Robin. "It has."

Winnie-the-Pooh

1

"Pooh, did you see me swimming? That's called swimming, what I was doing."

Winnie-the-Pooh

2

All Rabbit's friends-and-relations spread themselves about on the grass, and waited hopefully in case anybody spoke to them, or dropped anything, or asked them the time.

Winnie-the-Pooh

3

Rabbit said, "Ah, Eeyore," in the voice of one who would be saying "Good-bye" in about two more minutes.

The House At Pooh Corner

4

"You don't always want to be miserable on my birthday, do you?"

Winnie-the-Pooh

5

I think I am a Muffin Man. I haven't got a
  bell,
I haven't got the muffin things that muffin people
  sell.
Now We Are Six

6

"Look at the birthday cake. Candles and pink sugar."
Winnie-the-Pooh

7

Owl was explaining that in a case of Sudden and
Temporary Immersion the Important Thing was to keep
the Head Above Water. *Winnie-the-Pooh*

8

His arms were so stiff from holding on to the string of
the balloon all that time that they stayed up straight in
the air for more than a week. *Winnie-the-Pooh*

9

"Well," said Pooh, "it's the middle of the night, which is a good time for going to sleep."

The House At Pooh Corner

10

Christopher Robin began to tell Pooh about some of the things: People called Kings and Queens and something called Factors, and a place called Europe.

The House At Pooh Corner

11

These are my two drops of rain
Waiting on the window-pane.

Now We Are Six

12

And all the time Winnie-the-Pooh had been trying to get the honey-jar off his head. *Winnie-the-Pooh*

13

What shall we do about
  poor little Tigger?
If he never eats nothing he'll
  never get bigger.
The House At Pooh Corner

14

The verse beginning "O gallant Piglet" seemed to him a
very thoughtful way of beginning a piece of poetry.
The House At Pooh Corner

15

"We can't all, and some of us don't. That's all there is
to it."
Winnie-the-Pooh

16

Piglet was so proud that he would have called out
"Look at *me!*" if he hadn't been afraid that Pooh and
Owl would let go of their end of the string and look
at him. *The House At Pooh Corner*

17

Winnie-the-Pooh went to a very muddy place that he
knew of, and rolled and rolled until he was black all
over.   *Winnie-the-Pooh*

18

Rabbit never minded saying things again.
                          The House At Pooh Corner

19

They walked on, thinking of This and That, and
by-and-by they came to an enchanted place on the very
top of the Forest called Galleons Lap.
                          The House At Pooh Corner

20

"The atmospheric conditions have been very
unfavourable lately," said Owl.
                                    Winnie-the-Pooh

21

"You don't mind my asking," Eeyore went on, "but what colour was this balloon when it—when it *was* a balloon?"

Winnie-the-Pooh

22

"Let's frighten the dragons," I said to Pooh. "That's right," said Pooh to Me.

Now We Are Six

23

"This party," said Christopher Robin, "is a party because of what someone did, and we all know who it was."

Winnie-the-Pooh

24

Piglet was so excited at the idea of being Useful that he forgot to be frightened any more.   *Winnie-the-Pooh*

25

Christopher Robin came down from the Forest, feeling all sunny and careless, and just as if twice nineteen didn't matter a bit. *The House At Pooh Corner*

26

"We wake up one morning and, what do we find? We find a Strange Animal among us." *Winnie-the-Pooh*

27

"Balloon?" said Eeyore. "One of those big coloured things you blow up?" *Winnie-the-Pooh*

28

I often wish I were a King,
And then I could do anything.
When We Were Very Young

29

It wasn't much good having anything exciting like floods, if you couldn't share them with somebody.

Winnie-the-Pooh

30

"Being fine today doesn't Mean Anything," said Eeyore. "It's just a small piece of weather."

The House At Pooh Corner

31

At these encouraging words Piglet felt quite happy again, and decided not to be a Sailor after all.

The House At Pooh Corner

September

"After all," said Rabbit to himself, "Christopher Robin depends on Me. He's fond of Pooh and Piglet and Eeyore, and so am I, but they haven't any Brain. Not to notice. And he respects Owl, because you can't help respecting anybody who can spell TUESDAY, even if he doesn't spell it right; but spelling isn't everything. There are days when spelling Tuesday simply doesn't count."

The House At Pooh Corner

1

A hum came suddenly into his head, which seemed to him a Good Hum, such as is Hummed Hopefully to Others. *The House At Pooh Corner*

2

He tried Counting Sheep, and, as that was no good, he tried counting Heffalumps. And that was worse. *Winnie-the-Pooh*

3

He took a stick and touched Pooh on the shoulder, and said, "Rise, Sir Pooh de Bear, most faithful of all my Knights." *The House At Pooh Corner*

4

Rabbit went on to say that Kangas were only Fierce during the winter months. *Winnie-the-Pooh*

5

There lives an old man at the top of the street,
And the end of his beard reaches down to his feet.
When We Were Very Young

6

As soon as he saw the Big Boots, Pooh knew that an Adventure was going to happen.

Winnie-the-Pooh

7

"I generally have a small something about now—" and he looked wistfully at the cupboard.

Winnie-the-Pooh

8

"It isn't a growl, and it isn't a purr, and it isn't a bark, and it isn't the noise-you-make-before-beginning-a-piece-of-poetry."
The House At Pooh Corner

9

Binker—what I call him—is a secret of my own,
And Binker is the reason why I never feel alone.

Now We Are Six

10

With one last look back in his mind at all the happy hours he had spent in the Forest *not* being pulled up to the ceiling by a piece of string, Piglet nodded bravely.

The House At Pooh Corner

11

Piglet still felt that to be underneath a Very Good Dropper would be a Mistake.

The House At Pooh Corner

12

At last Owl's head came out and said "Go away, I'm thinking—oh, it's you?" which was how he always began.

The House At Pooh Corner

13

Christopher Robin
Got up in the morning,
The sneezles had vanished away.
Now We Are Six

14

"I *think* Heffalumps come if you whistle."
Winnie-the-Pooh

15

He was walking along gaily, wondering what everybody else was doing, and what it felt like, being somebody else.
Winnie-the-Pooh

16

Christopher Robin said, "Silly old Bear," in such a loving voice that everybody felt quite hopeful again.
Winnie-the-Pooh

17

"There is no hurry. We shall get there some day."
The House At Pooh Corner

18

"You can't help respecting anybody who can spell
TUESDAY, even if he doesn't spell it right."
The House At Pooh Corner

19

The Sun was still in bed, but there was a lightness in
the sky over the Hundred Acre Wood which seemed to
show that it was waking up.   *Winnie-the-Pooh*

20

When Christopher Robin had helped them out of the
Gravel Pit, they all went off together hand-in-hand.
The House At Pooh Corner

21

Christopher Robin banged on the table with his spoon, and everybody stopped talking. *Winnie-the-Pooh*

22

Oh, Daddy is clever, he's a clever sort of man,
And Mummy is the best since the world began.

Now We Are Six

23

He thought, "I haven't seen Roo for a long time, and if I don't see him today it will be a still longer time."

The House At Pooh Corner

24

"Eeyore, who is a friend of mine, has lost his tail. And he's Moping about it." *Winnie-the-Pooh*

25

Owl looked at him, and wondered whether to push him off the tree.   *The House At Pooh Corner*

26

Pooh was walking round and round in a circle, thinking of something else.   *Winnie-the-Pooh*

27

It is well known that, if One of the Fiercer Animals is Deprived of Its Young, it becomes as fierce as Two of the Fiercer Animals.   *Winnie-the-Pooh*

28

"I had a Very Important Missage sent me in a bottle, and owing to having got some water in my eyes, I couldn't read it."   *Winnie-the-Pooh*

29

"We've come to wish you a Very Happy Thursday,"
said Pooh.   *The House At Pooh Corner*

30

As soon as he woke up he felt important, as if
everything depended upon him.
                              The House At Pooh Corner

October

Pooh started to climb out of the hole. He pulled with his front paws, and pushed with his back paws, and in a little while his nose was out in the open again . . . and then his ears . . . and then his front paws . . . and then his shoulders . . . and then——

"Oh, help!" said Pooh. "I'd better go back."

"Oh, bother!" said Pooh. "I shall have to go on."

Winnie-the-Pooh

1

"I *think* that I have just remembered something that I forgot to do yesterday and shan't be able to do tomorrow."

Winnie-the-Pooh

2

"You ought to see that bird from here," said Rabbit. "Unless it's a fish."

Winnie-the-Pooh

3

In a corner of the room, the table-cloth began to wriggle.

The House At Pooh Corner

4

In a corner of the bedroom is a great big curtain,
Someone lives behind it, but I don't know who.

When We Were Very Young

5

It sounded to him like a riddle, and he was never much good at riddles, being a Bear of Very Little Brain.

Winnie-the-Pooh

6

When he thought of all the honey the bees wouldn't be making, a cold and misty day always made him feel sorry for them. *The House At Pooh Corner*

7

"Ha-ha," said Eeyore bitterly. "Merriment and what-not. Don't apologize. It's just what *would* happen." *The House At Pooh Corner*

8

"It's a Missage," he said to himself, "that's what it is."

Winnie-the-Pooh

9

Halfway up the stairs isn't up and isn't down.
It isn't in the nursery,
It isn't in the town.

When We Were Very Young

10

Everybody said "How-do-you-do" to Eeyore, and
Eeyore said that he didn't.

The House At Pooh Corner

11

"I've been thinking," said Pooh, "and I think——"
"No," said Rabbit. "Don't."

The House At Pooh Corner

12

"All the Poetry in the Forest has been written by Pooh,
a Bear with a Pleasing Manner but a Positively Startling
Lack of Brain."

The House At Pooh Corner

13

Then he began to think of all the things Christopher Robin would want to tell him when he came back from wherever he was going to.

The House At Pooh Corner

14

They all went off to discover the Pole, Owl and Piglet and Rabbit and all.

Winnie-the-Pooh

15

"It is either Two Woozles and one, as it might be, Wizzle, or Two, as it might be, Wizzles and one, if so it is, Woozle."

Winnie-the-Pooh

16

Much as he loved Pooh, he really had more brain than Pooh.

The House At Pooh Corner

17

They sighed and got up; and when they had taken a few gorse prickles out of themselves they sat down again.

Winnie-the-Pooh

18

He saw at once that what they were going to do to Tigger was a good thing to do. *The House At Pooh Corner*

19

Tigger made exploring noises with his tongue and considering noises, and what-have-we-got-*here* noises.

The House At Pooh Corner

20

Pooh was saying to himself, "If only I could *think* of something!" *Winnie-the-Pooh*

21

"Oh, help!" said Pooh. "I'd better go back."
Winnie-the-Pooh

22

He wondered if being a Faithful Knight meant that you just went on being faithful without being told things.
The House At Pooh Corner

23

Let it rain!
Who cares?
I've a train
Upstairs.
Now We Are Six

24

The last and smallest friend-and-relation was so upset that he buried himself head downwards in a crack in the ground.
Winnie-the-Pooh

25

"Did I fall on you, Piglet? I didn't mean to."
"I didn't mean to be underneath."
The House At Pooh Corner

26

Every one says, "Run along,
There's a little darling!"
If I'm a little darling, why don't they run with me?
Now We Are Six

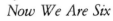

27

He went into his house and drew a picture of Pooh
going a long walk.   *The House At Pooh Corner*

28

If you look round and see a Very Fierce Heffalump
looking down at you, sometimes you forget what you
were going to say.   *The House At Pooh Corner*

29

Has anybody seen my mouse?

I opened his box for half a minute,
Just to make sure he was really in it.
When We Were Very Young

30

And then, suddenly, he remembered. He had eaten
Eeyore's birthday present! *Winnie-the-Pooh*

31

And it was eleven o'clock. Which was Time-for-a-
little-something. . . .
The House At Pooh Corner

November

"Hallo!" said Piglet, "what are *you* doing?"

"Hunting," said Pooh.

"Hunting what?"

"Tracking something," said Winnie-the-Pooh very mysteriously.

"Tracking what?" said Piglet, coming closer.

"That's just what I ask myself. I ask myself, What?"

"What do you think you'll answer?"

"I shall have to wait until I catch up with it," said Winnie-the-Pooh.

Winnie-the-Pooh

1

"What does the North Pole *look* like. I suppose it's just a pole stuck in the ground?"
Winnie-the-Pooh

2

He would go up very quietly to the Six Pine Trees now, peep very cautiously into the Trap, and see if there *was* a Heffalump there.
Winnie-the-Pooh

3

"It isn't so Hot in my field. Quite-between-ourselves-and-don't-tell-anybody, it's Cold."
The House At Pooh Corner

4

It seemed to Pooh to be one of the best songs he had ever sung. So he went on singing it.
The House At Pooh Corner

5

Christopher Robin went back to lunch with his friends Pooh and Piglet, and on the way they told him of the Awful Mistake they had made.

The House At Pooh Corner

6

Pooh always liked a little something at eleven o'clock in the morning. *Winnie-the-Pooh*

7

I think I am a Puppy,
so I'm hanging out my tongue.
Now We Are Six

8

By this time they were getting near Eeyore's Gloomy Place, which was where he lived.

The House At Pooh Corner

9

The Doctor said, "Tut! It's another attack!"
And ordered him Milk and Massage-of-the-back.
When We Were Very Young

10

Rabbit hurried on by the edge of the Hundred Acre Wood, feeling more important every minute.
The House At Pooh Corner

11

It was the first party to which Roo had ever been, and he was very excited. *Winnie-the-Pooh*

12

"Me having a real birthday?"
"Yes, Eeyore, and I've brought you a present."
Winnie-the-Pooh

13

If I had a ship,
I'd sail my ship,
I'd sail my ship
Through Eastern seas.
When We Were Very Young

14

If I were a bear,
  And a big bear too,
I shouldn't much care
  If it froze or snew.
  Now We Are Six

15

He jumped up and down once or twice in an exercising sort of way. *Winnie-the-Pooh*

16

Piglet made a squeaky Roo-noise from the bottom of Kanga's pocket. *Winnie-the-Pooh*

17

"If they are having a joke with me, I will have a joke with them."   *Winnie-the-Pooh*

18

"However," Eeyore said, brightening up a little, "we haven't had an earthquake lately."

The House At Pooh Corner

19

"Kanga, I see the time has come to spleak painly."

Winnie-the-Pooh

20

Christopher Robin had spent the morning indoors going to Africa and back.   *The House At Pooh Corner*

21

"This writing business. Pencils and what-not. Over-rated, if you ask me."

Winnie-the-Pooh

22

Piglet jumped six inches in the air with Surprise and Anxiety, but Pooh went on dreaming.

The House At Pooh Corner

23

"If anybody wants to clap," said Eeyore, "now is the time to do it." *The House At Pooh Corner*

24

Pooh, who had decided to be a Kanga, was practising jumps.

Winnie-the-Pooh

25

"Hallo!" said Piglet, "what are *you* doing?"

"Tracking something," said Winnie-the-Pooh very mysteriously. *Winnie-the-Pooh*

26

What is the matter with Mary Jane?
She's perfectly well and she hasn't a pain. *When We Were Very Young*

27

"I *love* jumping," said Roo. "Let's see who can jump farthest, you or me." *The House At Pooh Corner*

28

It was the only place in the Forest where you could sit down carelessly. *The House At Pooh Corner*

29

And then Piglet did a Noble Thing, and he did it in a sort of dream.

The House At Pooh Corner

30

"They haven't got Brains, any of them, only grey fluff that's blown into their heads by mistake."

The House At Pooh Corner

December

"When you wake up in the morning, Pooh," said Piglet at last, "what's the first thing you say to yourself?"

"What's for breakfast?" said Pooh. "What do *you* say, Piglet?"

"I say, I wonder what's going to happen exciting *today?*" said Piglet.

Pooh nodded thoughtfully.

"It's the same thing," he said.

Winnie-the-Pooh

1

"Good morning, Pooh Bear," said Eeyore gloomily. "If it *is* a good morning," he said.   *Winnie-the-Pooh*

2

All sorts and conditions
Of famous physicians
Came hurrying round
At a run.

Now We Are Six

3

They were out of the snow now, but it was very cold, and to keep themselves warm they sang Pooh's song right through six times.

The House At Pooh Corner

4

I'm a great big lion in my cage,
        And I often frighten Nanny with a roar.

When We Were Very Young

5

"I wonder what's going to happen exciting *today?*"
said Piglet.   *Winnie-the-Pooh*

6

He could read quite comfortably when you weren't
looking over his shoulder and saying "Well?" all
the time.   *The House At Pooh Corner*

7

One fine winter's day when Piglet was brushing away
the snow in front of his house, he happened to look up,
and there was Winnie-the-Pooh.   *Winnie-the-Pooh*

8

"We will build an Eeyore House with sticks at Pooh
Corner for Eeyore."   *The House At Pooh Corner*

9

Tigger had been bouncing in front of them all this time, turning round every now and then to ask, "Is this the way?"
The House At Pooh Corner

10

Where am I going? I don't quite know.
What does it matter where people go?
When We Were Very Young

11

He thought that he would like to be the first one to give a present, just as if he had thought of it without being told by anybody.
Winnie-the-Pooh

12

"It's all very well for Jumping Animals like Kangas, but it's quite different for Swimming Animals like Tiggers."
The House At Pooh Corner

13

Looking very calm, very dignified, with his legs in the air, came Eeyore from beneath the bridge.

The House At Pooh Corner

14

In after-years he liked to think that he had been in Very Great Danger during the Terrible Flood.

Winnie-the-Pooh

15

"What does Crustimoney Proseedcake mean?"

Winnie-the-Pooh

16

"Ah!" said Eeyore. "A mistake, no doubt, but still, I shall come. Only don't blame *me* if it rains."

Winnie-the-Pooh

17

That's all that I know of the three little foxes
Who kept their handkerchiefs in cardboard boxes.
When We Were Very Young

18

"People come and go in this Forest, and they say, 'It's only Eeyore, so it doesn't count.'"
The House At Pooh Corner

19

Winnie-the-Pooh read the two notices very carefully, first from left to right, and afterwards from right to left.
Winnie-the-Pooh

20

"What happens when the Heffalump comes?" asked Piglet tremblingly.
The House At Pooh Corner

21

Sitting there they could see the whole world spread out until it reached the sky. *The House At Pooh Corner*

22

Our Teddy Bear is short and fat
Which is not to be wondered at.
When We Were Very Young

23

Before he knew where he was, Piglet was in the bath, and Kanga was scrubbing him firmly with a large lathery flannel. *Winnie-the-Pooh*

24

"I want some crackers,
    And I want some candy;
I think a box of chocolates
    Would come in handy."
Now We Are Six

25

But every year at Christmas,
    While minstrels stood about,
He stole away upstairs and hung
    A hopeful stocking out.
        Now We Are Six

26

"I'm not going to do Nothing any more."
   "Never again?"
   "Well, not so much. They don't let you."
        The House At Pooh Corner

27

Pooh and Piglet walked home thoughtfully together in
the golden evening.   *Winnie-the-Pooh*

28

And he wanted some nets, or a line and some hooks
For the turtles and things which you read of in books.
        Now We Are Six

29

But now I am Six, I'm as clever as clever.
So I think I'll be six now for ever and ever.

Now We Are Six

30

"Pooh, *promise* you won't forget about me, ever. Not even when I'm a hundred."

The House At Pooh Corner

31

In that enchanted place on the top of the Forest, a little boy and his Bear will always be playing.

The House At Pooh Corner